For Charlie —
January 23, 1980 —
from Grandma —

Happy Birthday !!!

Curly and
the Wild Boar

Curly and the Wild Boar

by Fred Gipson

Illustrations by Ronald Himler

Harper & Row, Publishers
New York, Hagerstown, San Francisco, London

CURLY AND THE WILD BOAR
FIRST EDITION

Library of Congress Cataloging in Publication Data
Gipson, Frederick Benjamin, 1908–1973
    Curly and the wild boar.

    SUMMARY: A young boy repeatedly puts himself in danger
in his determination to kill the wild boar that has
destroyed his prize watermelon.
    [1. Country Life—Fiction]   I. Himler, Ronald.   II. Title.
PZ7.C4393Cu   1979   [Fic]   77-25644
ISBN 0-06-022014-7
ISBN 0-06-022015-5 lib. bdg.

For the people of Mason County, Texas,
who were the inspiration of his tales and talents.

CONTENTS

One

IT was sure a pretty morning, too pretty for a man to be on the lookout for trouble. And trouble was clear beyond the edge of Catfish Waggoner's thinking as he picked his way down the brush-lined trail toward his favorite fishing hole under a sandstone cliff on Wild Onion Creek.

The man felt the warmth of the early morning sun on his freckled face and hands. He smelled the fresh, pungent scent of bee myrtle flowering white after recent rains. He saw the grass greening on the rock-littered hill slopes. He heard the demanding call of a bobwhite quail and the resounding gobble of a wild turkey far off in the hills. And what he thought about was what he generally thought about when his mind was at ease. He thought about catfish.

The evening before, he and his older boy, Shinnery Red, had set out a trotline in the pool under the cliff. They'd baited it after sundown, using the finest bait the Almighty ever provided for luring catfish to a hook—the brown, finger-long, skin-pinching hellgrammites. They had found the hell-grammites under embedded rocks over which the shoaling creek waters foamed white farther down-stream.

Then had followed a real "catfish night," quiet, warm, and still, with no moonlight to reveal his baits to the robber gars and turtles. And just before daylight, a little flurry of rain had fallen, which was bound to have quickened the blood and aroused the appetite of any catfish ordinarily too lazy-fat to stir from his underwater nest.

What with such tempting baits and such ideal weather, Catfish didn't see how he could keep from snagging enough catfish to fill a tow sack—and he carried a tow sack along with him, just in case.

In fact, the thoughts of the pumpkin-bellied man were so far from trouble that he threw back his head and burst into song. His cracked, twangy voice wasn't what you'd call pretty, but it was stout. It startled the calling bobwhite into silence. It stampeded a little bunch of deer from a live-oak thicket. It so intrigued a *paisano* that the leggy gray bird came running, to pace along the trail ahead of the old man, now and then looking back over its shoulder with its topknot raised, obviously wondering what in the world all the commotion was about.

[4]

Catfish sang:

"And oh, what a weeping and wailing,
As the lost ones told of their fate;
They cried in the rocks in the mountains;
They prayed, but their prayers were too late."

Some people feel that when you are at peace with the world, you ought to sing happy, lilting songs, but Catfish Waggoner wasn't one of them. He liked the lonesome, hurting kind of music, full of misery and heartache; and now he smiled in real pleasure at the way the canyon echoes came alive and wailed back at him in doleful refrain.

His smile grew broader as he scrambled down off the last rock ledge and came in sight of the water. The near end of his trotline was tied to the springy branch of a willow growing beside the pool; and the way that branch twitched and jerked was enough to give a catfisherman heart failure.

"I knowed it!" he shouted jubilantly. "Any catfish wouldn't bite last night is bound to be laid up with a broke back!"

Quickly, he shucked out of his hat, shoes, pants, and shirt. But even out here where there was nobody but him and the wild creatures, he was too modest to strip down to the raw. He entered the water still clad in the red-handled "union suit" drawers that he wore winter and summer. He caught hold of the surging trotline and followed it,

[5]

hand over hand, out toward the middle of the limpid pool.

Eagerness rode him so hard that he didn't get far before he had to stop and raise the line to see what he'd caught. And the weight of the line was such that he had to lift it above his head to bring the nearest fish to the surface.

But the effort was worth it. Out of the water rose the flat head of a blue cat, with its back-sweeping whiskers and gaping gill flaps. And the size of that head was enough to take the man's breath away.

It was while he still stood there in water up to his armpits, round-eyed with wonder, his mouth hanging open like a flytrap, that he got his first warning that trouble was on the prowl.

From his cornfield, which lay on the hill slope above the cliff, came a sudden high-pitched screeching and howling. The sound gave Catfish the cold chills. He recognized the voice instantly. It belonged to his twelve-year-old son Curly, and Curly was in trouble!

For a moment, Catfish stood holding the trotline aloft, torn between an instinctive urge to go to Curly's aid and an almost overwhelming desire to land the biggest catfish he'd ever hooked in a long life of catfishing.

Then the catfish flounced, spanking the water with a mighty forked tail; at the same instant,

[7]

Catfish dropped the trotline and swam frantically past the fish toward the far bank.

He slipped and scrambled and skinned a shinbone against the rock ledge as he struggled up out of the water. He ran, dripping, along the ledge under the cliff toward the trail that led up out of the creek to his corn patch. His belly jostled. Sharp-edged rocks cut his bare feet. His mind wheeled in circles, thinking wild thoughts—*Curly's been snake-bit! He's been hog-cut. He's been mule-kicked. He's fell in a hole and broke both his pore little legs!*

Catfish struck the trail and went puffing up the steep slope. Before he was halfway to the top, his heaving lungs were on fire and he was blaming himself for all the whiskey he'd drunk and all the tobacco he'd smoked, bad habits that had cut back his wind, so that now it looked like he was sure to give out before he could ever save his baby boy from whatever horrible thing had him uttering such howls of agony.

Two

THERE was one thing you could say about Catfish Waggoner's skinny, rusty-headed, freckle-faced baby boy Curly: there were no halfway measures about him. Let him start a fist fight or a rat killing, it was all the same. He went at either one whole hog, with no holds barred. And this applied to his throwing a spoiled brat's mad fit.

This morning, out in the middle of his daddy's corn patch, Curly was throwing himself a fit to end all fits. He lay flat on his stomach in a tangle of trampled watermelon vines and beat the red earth with clenched fists. He kicked it with the toes of his boots. He wept tears into the dirt. One minute, he'd squawl out like a bobcat in a steel trap, and the next, he'd cut loose with a string of vile words that he sure hadn't picked up around any Sunday school class.

He was still going loud and strong when his daddy came charging through the corn, knocking

[9]

roasting ears loose from the stalks like a runaway horse.

Catfish broke into the opening where Curly's two-row watermelon patch ran the full length of the field. There the man halted his charge and stood panting, staring down at his enraged off-spring. The wild protective urge that had panicked him back there at the creek gradually died out, replaced first by bewilderment, then disgust.

When at last he could get back breath enough to speak, Catfish exploded.

"Dog take it, Curly! What in the tarnation is this all about, anyhow?"

He reached down with a callused hand to grasp Curly by his shirt collar and yank him to his feet. Curly jerked free and glared at his father out of desperate, tear-filled eyes.

Catfish said, "Now, if you ain't a purty sight! Wallering in the dirt like a five-year-old with con-niption fits. Squawling like you'd run yourself through with a butcher knife. Making me maybe lose the biggest catfish I ever hoped to catch. A regular lollapalooza if I ever saw one."

Curly swiped at the teary mud on his cheeks with his shirt sleeve, and his chin quivered.

"You and your catfish!" he charged bitterly. He waved an arm dramatically and his small-boy's voice cracked and rose shrilly. "Just look at that!"

Catfish lifted a bare foot to extract several goathead burs buried in the tender flesh of a big toe. He screwed his face up and grunted with pain with each extraction. When finally he got around to looking to where Curly pointed, his eyes widened. All up and down the melon rows, he could see vines that had been shoved aside and trampled on. Here and there, the rattlesnake stripes of a half-grown melon still gleamed in the sun. But where once there had been huge melons ripening among the vines, now those melons were reduced to shattered, trampled bits of rind, scattered seeds, and scraps of luscious red melon heart gradually soaking into the ground.

"Why—why, thunderation!" he exclaimed. "There's been hogs in my corn patch. Be dog, if there ain't!"

"In your corn!" shrieked the outraged Curly. "What about my watermelons? What about my show melon? The one I aimed to take the prize with at the county fair?"

Curly burst into sobs all over again.

Immediately, Catfish was all sympathy and kindness. He reached out and put a comforting arm around Curly's thin shoulders. He drew the boy up close against his wet red underwear. "Now, now," he said clumsily. "Don't take it so hard, Curly."

Curly pulled away from him. "Whatta you mean, don't take it so hard?" he flared. "Why, confound it, I been nursing my prize melon like a baby. I

[11]

packed a thousand buckets of water up the hill from the creek to keep it going through the dry spells. I hoed it and the rest of the vines when I could have been fishing or bobcat-hunting. I slept with that melon and sometimes prayed for it. Had it weighing better'n eighty pounds. And now look at it. Et up in five minutes by one fence-breaking wild hog!"

Curly glared bitterly at his father, as if the old man were responsible for his loss.

Catfish looked helplessly around, somehow feeling guilty. "Yeah, I know, son," he finally said. "I been watching you take care of that big melon. I knowed you had your heart set on winning the blue ribbon with it." He heaved a big quivering sigh. "But that's how the wind blows sometimes. A body's luck runs out on him, and there ain't one frazzling thing he can do about it. Maybe next year—"

"Who said there ain't nothing I can do about it?" Curly broke in furiously. "I can kill the dang hog what done it. I'll do it, too. I'll run him to ground and cut piggin' strings out of his ornery hide. I'll slit his throat and leave him for the buzzards to pick clean. I'll—"

"Now, now, hold on there," Catfish broke in. "Tuck in your shirttail, baby. You got to learn to halter your temper and bear trouble like a man."

"Baby!" Curly shrieked. "You figure I'm still a

baby, huh? Well, I'll show you how much of a baby I am. I'll bring you a wad of piggin' strings big enough to tie down a whole herd of calves. And I'll cut them out of the hide of a melon-stealing hog when I do it!"

Following this dire threat, the infuriated Curly wheeled and tore out through the corn in a hard run, headed for the house.

Catfish opened his mouth to call him back, then closed it without uttering a word. What was the use, he asked himself. He never had been able to control his hot-headed boys. Either one could out-think, outtalk, and outdo him from the word go, and they'd been that way, it seemed like, from the time they had quit wearing diapers.

Catfish stood there in his wet drawers, scratching moodily while he stared down at the paint-red earth—the best corn- and watermelon-growing dirt in the country—and worried about Curly and his hair-trigger temper. The boy always had been touchy as a teased snake, even worse than his brother, Shinnery Red. And right now, at twenty, Shinnery Red was ready at the drop of a hat to fist-fight all over a two-acre piece of ground. And to get things going, he'd drop the hat himself.

Catfish sighed and shook his head. When it came to managing his boys, he felt as helpless as a wooden-legged widow at a square dance. His woman, Laurie, had died at Curly's birth, and since that time, Catfish had tried to be both mother and father to the boys; but it looked like he'd made a frazzling poor job of it.

"Now, neither boy," he muttered to himself, "is what you'd call downright trouble-hunting mean. It's just that they're so hot-tempered and butt-headed. Harder to manage than a one-eyed mule in fly time!"

Still troubled, Catfish picked his way out of the cornfield and back down the rocky trail toward the catfish hole; and now it seemed like, at every third step, his tender bare feet picked up another bur or mesquite thorn or got another chunk of hide scraped off against a rock. By the time he'd reached his trotline again, he was convinced that he'd be a pencil-selling cripple for the rest of his life.

And just as he'd expected, when he waded out and lifted up his trotline, all he had left on his staging was a bare hook with a straightened-out shank. His big blue cat was gone.

There were plenty of smaller catfish still on the line, and Catfish sacked them; but his heart wasn't in it. He was too dejected by the loss of that big one and too troubled by thoughts of what might happen to Curly if the kid took out after that wild hog, like he'd threatened. Judging from the size of the tracks among the melons, Catfish knew that hog had been a big one; and any hog that managed to live wild in the hills till he got full-grown was bound to be a dangerous customer. Too dangerous for a shirttail kid to tamper with.

Catfish still wore across the right cheek of his rump a long, ugly scar marking the place where a wild sow's tusk had laid his flesh open to the bone. And it had happened so quickly—when he'd thought he was clear out of the sow's reach!

He waded ashore with his sack of catfish. He sat down and was trying to cram his bruised wet feet into ragged, run-over boots when he jerked around at the sound of crashing brush and iron-shod hoofs popping the rocks.

It was Curly, coming down the trail from the house. He was mounted on a high-headed young black horse that Shinnery Red called Midnight. He had the snorty black quirted into a dead run and was calling the dogs.

Aghast, Catfish lunged to his feet. "Curly!" he cried out. "I've told you not to saddle that black. He ain't half broke, and mean as all get out!"

He knew Curly heard him, for the kid looked his way as he tore past. But Curly didn't answer. He just came charging on down the slope and put Midnight into the shallow creek crossing without ever slackening pace. Sheets of water flew in all directions.

Catfish's heart leaped into his throat. "Look out!" he screamed. "Them creek rocks is slick!"

One misstep on those treacherous rocks, and Midnight would turn a wildcat. In his mind, Catfish could already see it happening, with Curly landing under the full weight of the horse, where every bone in his body would be broken.

Only it didn't happen that way. The sure-footed Midnight plunged on through the shallows and went tearing up the opposite slope in a buck-jumping run that had Curly's loose shirttail flopping in the wind.

Two of Catfish's dogs led the run—Coalie, the black shepherd, and Liverpill, the lemon-spotted hound. Behind the horse raced Half-Pint, the bench-legged feist, his tail curled up so tight with excitement that it all but had his hind feet lifted off the ground. Eager for a chase, all three dogs were yipping and yelping and flinging high-headed looks around, trying to locate what sort of varmint Curly was after.

His mind a turmoil of doubts and fears, Catfish stared helplessly after the wild-riding Curly and felt an urge to weep. Then he turned at a sound that came from up the creek. It was Shinnery Red, riding toward him on a young bay horse that was wearing the saddle for the third time. At the sight, Catfish's troubled mind took on still another worry.

He didn't like the way that big stout bronc crab-walked toward him, all humped up under the saddle like he was afraid it might touch his back somewhere. The rascal held his head too low, and it was plain to see that he was searching under every bush for some terrible monster, like maybe a cottontail rabbit, to take a scare at. Then he'd come uncoupled and go pitching and bawling down that rocky creek bed, doing his dead level best to unload his rider. And while, so far, Shinnery Red had made good his brags about "riding anything that wore hair," still and all, the best bronc buster who ever forked a saddle got stacked sometimes. And sometimes they got killed.

But the big smiling rawboned Shinnery kept sweet-talking the bronc along in the quiet, reassuring voice that he used on fractious horses and skittish women. Finally he hauled back on the hackamore rope, pulling the bay to a halt near his father.

"Who lit a fire under Curly's tail?" he wanted to know.

Catfish told him what the trouble was and added, "And now Curly's throwed hisself such a big mad fit that I don't hardly know what to do with him."

Shinnery Red threw back his head and laughed in a way to make the bronc snort and sidle around.

"Why, there's no use in your doing nothing, Pa," he said. "Curly's all right. He'll grow up one of these days. Just like I done. If he don't break his neck first."

"That's just it," Catfish burst out. "Little feller

[18]

like him, he just might get his neck broke."

"I didn't," Shinnery Red pointed out. "And I was pretty bad about backing my ears and trying to charge hell with a bucket of water."

Catfish nodded soberly. "You was sure bronc-headed, all right," he agreed. "But then, you was always big and stout, Shinnery. When you bowed up, something had to give. But you take that Curly, now—he ain't no bigger'n a starved gopher. Let him tangle with some old scalawag hog, and he's liable to get cut all to pieces. Hurt and mad like he is over losing his prize watermelon, he's all fight and no judgment." Catfish looked up at his big capable son, his eyes pleading for help.

Shinnery Red grinned warmly down at him. "Now, Pa," he comforted, "you're all unstrung. Tell you what: why don't you go back up to the cabin and set with your jug for a spell. It'll help to calm your nerves."

"But what about Curly?" Catfish demanded.

"Leave Curly to me," Shinnery Red said. "I'll trail along after him and see that he don't get hog-et."

"But he's riding that Midnight horse!" Catfish persisted.

"Now, Pa," Shinnery Red chided. "You're just borrowing trouble. Curly can ride Midnight anywhere the high-headed rascal can go. Curly may

[19]

not be much for size, but he sticks to a saddle like a cocklebur to a cow's tail."

Shinnery Red hauled the stiff-necked bay horse around and rode off toward the creek crossing without giving Catfish a chance to argue further. The old man gazed after him, while a great warming rush of emotion—part relief and part pride—brought the start of tears to his eyes.

By dog, he told himself, *it sure is comforting to have a grown boy willing to take over problems too big and confusing for an old man.*

Catfish went back to stuffing his sore feet into his boots, shaking his head at the baffling complexities of life. How could anybody as uncertain and inadequate as he was have ever raised a son as sure of himself and as capable as Shinnery Red? It didn't make sense. You just name it, Catfish Waggoner couldn't do it. But his boy, Shinnery Red, could— and he could do it up right and proper, too.

With his mind settled on that score, Catfish soon put aside his worries about Curly and eventually got around to thinking about what he liked to think about: catfish.

There was bound to be some way, he told himself, that he could lure that big blue cat to the hook again. All he had to do was come up with some different and better kind of bait. The rascal would be too smart to take a hellgrammite again soon, anyway.

Three

AT the cornfield gate, Curly reined the fractious Midnight down to a prancing walk and rode alongside the net-wire fence his father had built around the patch of cleared ground to keep the goats and range hogs from depredating on his crops. Curly followed a game trail that wound through the brush, more or less paralleling the fence, but didn't bother to study the tracks in the trail. He kept his eyes on the fence. Somewhere, during the night, that wild hog had found or made a break in the fence, and Curly wanted to find the place. Then would be time enough to start searching for tracks.

The eager dogs couldn't wait, though. They'd known from the start, back there when Curly first called them from under the house, that there was a chase coming up. And now, all aroused, they were getting more and more impatient to get the chase started. They kept ranging in wide circles around Curly, their keen noses sifting out the scent of an opossum here, a deer there, or a raccoon somewhere else, and wondering all the time which scent it was that Curly wanted them to follow.

Then, right ahead of Curly, in the dew-wet sand of the trail, Liverpill caught the hot, fresh scent of bobcat. That was too much for the hound. Curly had chased bobcats before, and Liverpill figured this ought to be what they were after. He lifted his head and gave tongue, then took out through the brush, wringing a joyous tail and setting the hill echoes to clamoring with the wild ring of his trail voice.

Instantly, Coalie and Half-Pint streaked after him, the shepherd whimpering with eagerness, while Half-Pint set up a screeching that sounded as if somebody were whipping him out of a smoke-house with a blacksnake.

"Liverpill! Confound it! Come back here!"

Curly's voice was shrill with outrage. He slammed spurs into Midnight so suddenly that the horse snorted and exploded under him like a stick of dynamite. He leaped so high and so far that if Curly hadn't been every bit the bur-tight rider Shinnery Red said he was, he'd have been left in the top of a nearby live oak when the black came back to earth.

But by grabbing the horn, Curly held what he had and was sitting solid in his saddle when the black took off after the dogs, running like a scared cat across the rock-littered slope and knocking down what brush he couldn't dodge around. And all the time, Curly was yelling at the dogs to come back and grabbing at dead tree branches as he tore past them. He broke the wood off and hurled the sticks at Liverpill, threatening to break the fool hound's back in fourteen different places if he didn't quit running the wrong trail.

Driven on by the wild urge of the chase, Liverpill pretended not to hear. But when one of the whizzing sticks caught him a stinging blow across the rump, the hound couldn't very well ignore that. So he let out a startled yelp and managed to look terribly surprised and injured and innocent as Curly reined Midnight to a rearing halt beside him.

"You confounded butt-head!" Curly raged. "You better listen to me the next time I holler at you. You know dang well you heard me and you know dang well I didn't put you on that trail to start with!"

The hound tucked his tail and sank to his belly, cringing with guilt.

Coalie and Half-Pint tucked their tails and looked as sneaky as Liverpill.

Curly reined the panting Midnight around and started riding back toward the field. He called over his shoulder to the dogs, "All right, now. Come on—and pay me some mind the next time. It's a hog we're after—not no bobcat."

[23]

Relieved to find that Curly didn't plan to break their backs in fourteen different places right at this very moment, the dogs rose from their crouches and trotted meekly after him.

It was around on the far side of the corn patch that Curly found the break in the fence. Actually, it wasn't a break at all, just a place where runoff water from the field had cut a gully that ran under the net wire. Sometime in the past, Catfish had shoved a short log into the opening and covered it with dead brush, as a sort of blind; but none of this had fooled that melon-raiding hog. Curly could see signs in the damp red earth where the hog had shoved through the brush, rooted the log aside, then proceeded to crawl in under the fence. The same signs showed that, after raiding the melon patch, the hog had come back out the same way.

That was all Curly wanted to know. He leaped to the ground with a suddenness that startled Midnight. The horse snorted and shied away. Curly hauled him down with a heavy hand on the reins to show who was boss.

"You hold still!" he shouted furiously. "Before I pull your head clean off your shoulders."

Midnight held still.

Curly bent low over the hog tracks and called to the hound.

"All right, Liverpill," he said, pointing, "here's you a trail to run, and you dang well better hang with it, too. You lose it, and I'll tie knots in them long flop ears."

Liverpill paid no attention to the threat; he was too eager to run. He sniffed the tracks that Curly pointed to, caught the faint rank scent of hog, and took off, wringing his tail and bawling his mightiest.

Coalie and Half-Pint fell in after Liverpill. The shepherd didn't have the keen nose of the trail hound and wasn't for certain yet what they were trailing, but he had learned to depend on the hound. Half-Pint, who couldn't have smelled a hot buttered biscuit twenty feet away, didn't care what they were running. All he wanted was to get in on the excitement.

Curly mounted and reined the quivering black around and spurred him after the dogs.

The chase didn't last long. The dew was still on the ground, making the scent easy for Liverpill to follow. Also, the marauding razorback hadn't considered it worth the effort to travel far on a gorged stomach. After leaving the field, he'd wandered out into the brush a ways, then gradually worked his way around in a wide half circle to hole up in a live-oak and bee-brush thicket that stood against the west side of the field fence. There he'd bedded down in a cool shade to sleep off his melon-eating jag.

The boar roused up with a rumbling grunt as his

wary senses warned him that the bugling of the trail hound was drawing near. But he made no move to leave the thicket. He was an old boar, without fear, and wise with the caginess that comes of surviving in the wilds. He'd been chased by dogs before, and he knew this shadowy thicket was exactly the sort of tight nest he needed for making a standoff fight. That's why he'd bedded down there in the first place. So he backed his spindly rump up against the net-wire fence and stood his ground, massive head and shoulders faced toward the approaching threat. His little eyes were mean and wary, and low-voiced sounds of warning rumbled in his throat.

Hot on the boar's trail, Liverpill plunged headlong into the brush, with Coalie and Half-Pint running hard on his heels.

An explosive roar from inside the thicket warned the dogs just in time. All three put on the brakes so quickly that their feet plowed deep furrows in the leaf-littered soil before they could come to a halt and wheel away to safety. They had learned about crowding a vicious old tusker in a thicket where there wasn't room to make a quick retreat.

Tails tucked, they came tearing back out of the brush faster than they'd gone into it. And not more than three feet behind them charged the lanky black boar, roaring his wrath and popping his teeth

[26]

in a way to set all three dogs to yelping with terror.

The sight of Curly charging up on Midnight and shouting encouragement to the dogs halted the boar at the edge of the brush. He stood silent for an instant, considering the approaching rider and the baying dogs. Then he retreated, to take up his stand with his rump against the fence again. His stance, the fierce look in his eyes, and the long, rumbling roars issuing from his throat said just as plain as anybody's words, "Here I stand, right inside this thicket, and any boy, horse, or dog who thinks he can take me is welcome to make his try!"

Yet one glimpse at the wild hog convinced Curly that the old boar wasn't nearly as deadly as he tried to let on. That was because of the shape of the boar's tusks. They were the longest, most fearsome-looking tusks Curly had ever seen on a wild hog. But they were ivory-white freaks. The bottom ones curved down around his underjaw, while the upper ones hooked over in front of his eyes. They made the boar look as dangerous as a wild beast had a right to look. At the same time, they rendered the old battler virtually harmless.

As long as those tusks were, with the keen points curled in, the old boar couldn't have cut his mark on the side of a tree. He could thrust and stab all he pleased and he still couldn't break the hide on a dog.

The trouble was, the boar didn't know that he

wasn't dangerous, the dogs didn't know it, and Curly could whoop and holler till he got red in the face and still not convince hog or dogs of this simple fact.

"Hy-yah!" Curly yelled at the dogs. "Tie into him. He can't hurt you!"

But the dogs had their own private opinions about that. This was plain to note in the hysterical sound of their baying, in the way their bristles stood up along the fear-humped line of their backbones, in the way their lips curled back, baring their fangs.

By insistent urgings, Curly could get the dogs to rally closer around the hog, but getting them to charge the old tusker was something else. The dogs could think of fifty safer places to go than inside that thicket where the coughing roars of the embattled boar had even Midnight rearing and squealing and trying to run backwards.

But Curly kept after the dogs. "Go git him!" he shouted. "Tie into him and drag him out. I want that melon-eating rascal, and I aim to get him."

Curly took down his rope and ran out a loop. He rapped the snorting Midnight down one hind leg with the rope to set him up on his toes and make him behave himself. Then Curly cocked his loop, ready to latch on any time those fool dogs raked up nerve enough to bring the boar out into the open.

Half-Pint was the first to make a try. As far as size

went, Half-Pint didn't go very far; but when it came to grit and courage, the little curl-tailed dog had his full share. Or it could be he just had a bigger head than the others for ignorance and foolhardiness. Anyhow, he sneaked around and came in from one side while the razorback's attention was fixed on the bigger dogs out front.

Half-Pint crept close, waited till the raging boar was turned broadside to them, then lunged in. He grabbed for a ham-hold and got it. He sank his teeth in deeply, at the same time throwing his weight around in a manner calculated to drag the big hog off-balance.

The feist made a mighty pretty job of his catch, all right, but he hadn't reckoned with the net-wire fence beside him. His lunging body hit the taut wires and rebounded, killing the effect of his side-swinging drag.

The boar whirled on him with a coughing roar. Half-Pint screeched in mortal terror. The lightning-quick thrust of the old boar's tusks was meant to disembowel him, and the little dog knew it.

It was only the long, freakish curve of the ivory blades that saved the screeching feist. He was knocked ten feet to one side by the boar's slamming blow, but the murderous points of the tusks never touched him.

The boar pivoted to face the bigger dogs, now lunging in for an attack, and the feist got his feet under him. He didn't wait around for more. He quit the thicket on flying short legs, yipping frantically, with his tail gripping the underside of his belly.

"Hy-yaaaaaah! Git him!" Curly yelled, then had to fight the spooked Midnight to keep him from stampeding.

Meanwhile, a savage lunge of the old boar had knocked Coalie off his feet and sent him rolling. The screaming shepherd was uninjured but too scared to realize it.

The boar turned from Coalie. He saw the raging hound coming in beside the fence and made a run at him.

Liverpill barely escaped the fate of the others. He flung himself sideways, yelping in fear. The hog missed, and wires screeched in the rusty post staples all up and down the fence as the infuriated boar plowed head-on into the netting.

The hog lunged back to renew the attack, but suddenly couldn't. The upthrusting lick he'd made at the hound had run one of those long upper tusks through the fence. A wire had slipped inside the hook and the downpull of the hog's weight merely held it tighter. The big boar was trapped.

Four

CURLY leaped to the ground, paying no attention to Midnight, who snorted and ran backwards, trailing the bridle reins. The boy hurried into the thicket, grinning his triumph. He jerked a rawhide piggin' string from his belt. He had expected to have to rope the hog when the dogs brought him out, but this was better. With the boar already caught in the fence, all Curly had to do was throw the big helpless fighter and tie him down. Then he'd proceed to cut the melon-eating rascal's throat, just like he'd told his pa he would. He hollered at the raging dogs, who were gradually moving in on the boar.

"Hush up and come back out of there!" he commanded. "He's done caught himself."

The dogs didn't hush their baying, but it was no trouble to get them to move back out of the thicket. They hadn't wanted to go in there in the first place. They didn't trust that roaring boar hog. They wouldn't have trusted him if Curly had had all four of his feet bound and his mouth wrapped shut with baling wire.

Maybe it was Curly's shout that did it. Or maybe the old boar had just been too surprised at being caught to make any real effort at releasing himself. Anyhow, he suddenly flung himself backwards, shaking his head and throwing all of his two hundred pounds of lean, live weight against the one small strand of steel wire holding him.

The wire stretched, but held. The long, hooked tusk didn't. Curly heard a sound like the snapping of bone and halted in panic as he saw the boar lunge free and whirl about to charge him. And what froze the blood in the boy's veins was the sight of one of the boar's tusks. It had snapped off against the pull of the wire, leaving a four-inch splinter still set in the hog's jaw, and that splinter was as sharp-pointed and deadly as a bayonet.

Curly wasn't the sort to panic easily, but right now he was caught between a rock and a hard place. That roaring boar was already charging him, and for close-in fighting there is no animal that can move faster. The boy knew he couldn't outrun the hog, even on open ground. Here in thick brush, there was no hope of dodging to one side. He knew he had only one slim chance of getting out of this scrape alive, and he steeled himself to make the most of it.

Curly figured all this out in one flash of disconnected thought and hoped frantically that he had the nerve to stand hitched and not jump too soon.

The boar rushed the boy with an explosive roar.

With his heart pounding, Curly waited till the last possible instant. Then he leaped straight up, flinging his legs wide apart.

The boar swept under him, cutting high.

The broken splinter of tusk slashed through one of Curly's boot tops and into the flesh. Curly felt the sting of it, but didn't wait around to examine his wound. Instead, he charged straight ahead through a tangle of brush and flung himself bodily up on top of the net-wire fence.

Where Curly struck the fence was in the middle of a long span of wire between two cedar posts, but there was no time for changing places. Already the enraged boar had heeled about and was charging again.

Clinging to the top of the sagging wire, Curly jerked his feet up out of reach just in time. The hog hit the fence under him and rebounded. The wire, top-heavy with Curly's weight, swayed out over the hog, and for an instant, Curly knew the wild despair that comes of looking death square in the eye, with no hope of escape.

Then, as the hog came at him again, Curly felt the pendulous wire under him swinging back in the opposite direction. His body moved with terrifying slowness, it seemed to Curly, yet it did keep

[34]

ahead of the charging hog. Then it was out of reach of the monster, and Curly flung himself free.

The hog hit the wire fence again but didn't come through, and Curly landed flat on his back in a patch of sandburs that grew inside the field.

Instantly, Curly was on his feet and backing away from the fence, watching the hog. Bristles standing on end, the angry boar stood on the other side of the fence, watching Curly. The dogs hung back at a safe distance. They kept up a constant baying, but it was mostly bluff.

The frightened Midnight decided that he'd a whole lot rather be somewhere else, so he started for the house, holding his head high and sideways to keep from stepping on the dragging bridle reins.

"Whoa!" Curly shouted at the horse.

Midnight began walking faster.

"Whoa! Dang you!"

Curly started down his side of the fence at a trot, meaning to get ahead of the horse and climb over and stop him.

The irate boar ran alongside Curly, popping frothy teeth and daring the boy to climb back over.

Curly didn't take the dare. Instead, he picked up a fist-sized chunk of red sandstone. He hurled it through the wires, striking the boar in the ribs. The big hog roared, leaped aside, and charged Curly. The fence held him back, but the hog wouldn't leave. He was plenty riled and kept hunting a

[36]

break in the wire that would let him through to Curly.

Curly called on the dogs again then, whistling to them, talking it up big, urging them to make a catch. He had to get out of this cornfield and get his hands on Midnight before the fool black escaped to the house. Curly had made his brags about catching that hog, and if Midnight got away and showed up at the cabin wearing an empty saddle, Catfish and Shinnery Red would laugh Curly off the place. There would be no living with them for months.

"Catch him!" Curly yelled at the dogs. "Confound it! Tie into him and drag him down."

Urged on by Curly, the dogs crowded closer to the rumbling hog and bayed louder. But they didn't tie into him. They'd had one taste of that vicious old boar and they didn't particularly like his flavor.

Curly saw how it was and threw another temper fit. He screamed at the dogs. He screamed at Midnight. He screamed at the boar. Then he started running through the corn toward the field gate. If he ran fast enough, he might get ahead of Midnight and catch him as he started down the trail into the creek canyon.

He was fast enough, but he didn't catch the horse. When he vaulted over the fence close to the gate, he saw the black horse rounding the corner of the corn patch with the dogs and the boar hog trailing after. At the same time, he saw a thing that made his heart sink into his boots.

It was his big brother, Shinnery Red, riding toward him out of the brush. And that long-shanked, red-headed bronc buster was rocking and reeling in his saddle, bawling with laughter.

"Now, if that wasn't a sight to pop your eyeballs!" Shinnery Red whooped, pointing at Curly. "I just wish Pa could have seen it. Man, oh, man! Wait till I tell him how you rose and flew like a bird to the top of that fence. With that old boar hog cutting the grease outta the seat of your britches!" He slapped his leg. "I've been to three barbecues and four goat-ropings and never yet seen anything get so high behind in such a big hurry!"

Curly's momentary panic died. Anger turned his eyes the color of green glass chips reflecting the sunlight.

"Yeah," he drawled in a dangerous tone of voice. "I bet it was a funny sight. So funny, you just sat there in your saddle, laughing your fool head off and not turning a hand to help out."

"That's right," Shinnery Red said, wiping tears from his eyes. "I aimed for that old hog to learn you a lesson, boy. On how to hold down your hot temper."

Shinnery Red broke into new shouts of laughter, while Curly stood and glared at him. Curly's rage wasn't the small-boy mad-fit kind that it had been. This time, it was cold and calculating. He stopped staring at his brother and looked around him, searching till his eye lit on a short cedar stay that had fallen out of the fence. With a casual movement, he stepped over and picked up the seasoned stick of wood. He shook it once to get the feel of it, then whirled and flung it at his brother's head.

The startled Shinnery fell half out of the saddle, dodging the whizzing chunk of wood. Which was entirely too much for the snorty bay horse he straddled. All morning long, that bronc had been looking for a real good excuse to fall to pieces under his rider, and this seemed to him like the best he could hope to find. He snorted loud, bogged his head, and quit the earth with the saddle skirts popping.

Shinnery Red was a bronc rider in anybody's book. There was no question about that, even in Curly's mind. But right now the big rawboned rider was caught off guard and off-balance. He clawed frantically for leather to hold himself on with, and he got it. But the bawling, hard-pitching bay kept moving out from under him too fast. Shinnery Red never could quite catch up with the rascal. About the third or fourth jump, the bay shed his rider like a sack of salt, piling Shinnery Red up in a spiny tasajillo cactus bush. Then the wall-eyed creature took out down the trail toward the creek, still pitching and bawling and slinging saddle stirrups high in the air.

At this, the approaching Midnight decided he'd get in on the fun. He slung his head high and went to pitching off down the trail after the bay. This excited the dogs, who rushed after the runaway horses, baying them mightily. And the big boar, not understanding what all the commotion was about, stood and stared stupidly after them for a moment before deciding to call off his fight with Curly. He turned and faded into the brush, headed for a shady mudhole he knew about, where he meant to wallow around during the heat of the day.

Curly stood and watched his big brother gingerly extracting himself from the crushed tasajillo bush. Shinnery Red's weight had made a wreck of that bush, and the spiny cactus plant had pretty well made a wreck of Shinnery Red. He emerged as bristly as a startled porcupine. Spines were stuck into his shirt, into his rawhide chaps, into the seat of his pants, into his hands and face. But for the moment, it wasn't the hot-needle pain of those spines that concerned Shinnery Red. It was sight of that bay bronc pitching off down the canyon slope with an empty saddle.

The big redhead turned an angry look on his little brother. "Confound it, look what you've gone and done!" he shouted. "Spooked that horse out from under me. Now he'll think he can throw me again. Take me a month's hard work to get him gentled down to where I already had him."

"I'd bet on it," Curly said smugly. "I'd bet that, for the next week, you'll have to throw him and roll him into the saddle every time you try to ride him."

"Well, what'd you do it for?" Shinnery Red demanded.

Curly grinned maliciously. "I done it to learn *you* a lesson. Any big blowhard who'd set around and laugh while a wild boar hog is trying to cut his brother to scrap meat needs to learn a lesson or two."

Shinnery Red's face flamed red with anger. "Why, dang your ornery hide!" he flared. He lunged toward Curly, but halted suddenly with a gasp of pain, grabbing for the two-inch cactus spine stabbing him in the rear. He gasped again as he yanked the spine free.

With a jeering laugh, Curly turned and headed down the trail at a trot, following after the runaway horses.

Leaving his big brother there, virtually helpless until he'd pulled that mess of cactus spines out of his hide, gave Curly a big lift.

Five

THE catfish were butchered and put away in a sack of corn meal, ready for deep frying when dinnertime came. Now Catfish Waggoner sat out on his front gallery in a creaky rocking chair where the early morning breeze caressed him with a cooling touch. On the floor beside him sat his jug, handy to his reach, and repeated nibblings at the jug had washed from his mind all troubles and anxieties, leaving him warmly mellow and slightly weepy with the tragic joy of life.

Be dog, if it wasn't a pretty world he lived in. With the grass coming green on the hill slopes, the canyon ringing with sweet birdsong, the brush full of wild game, and the catfish biting like they couldn't wait.

A world as pretty as a body could imagine.

And then there were his boys. A pair to make a man walk in pride with the knowledge that they were his to love and enjoy. Maybe a bit broncheaded and high-handed, but who wanted lace-panty boys, ready to jump through themselves every time somebody hollered "froggy." No, sir. What a man wanted was boys with spirit, with the gumption to go ahead and do whatever they felt big enough to do, even if they sometimes had to walk over their own pa a little to get it done. Which was exactly the sort of boys he had. Wasn't a thing on earth Shinnery Red and Curly couldn't do, once they set their minds to do it. Not one dogged, frazzling thing.

With this conviction strong in his mind, Catfish reached for the jug and took another nip. The next instant, he'd lurched to his feet. He stood holding the jug in one hand and shading his eyes with the other, while from within him came a little frightened whimper of despair.

For there was no mistaking what he saw down there at the creek crossing. It was two wildly running horses, headed for the house, chased by three yipping dogs. And the sight of those two empty saddles, with loose stirrups flopping about, completely shattered Catfish's faith in the invincibility of his beloved sons. Now they were no longer young gods, striding mightily across the face of the earth. They were mere children, poor little helpless babies, who obviously had been cut to pieces by a wild hog or trampled to death under the hammering hoofs of man-killer horses.

Catfish left the gallery in a high run. He tore out

through the front-yard gate and down the trail toward the creek. Too stricken with a sense of calamity to remember his jug, he carried it with him, waving his free arm frantically about as he ran.

The frightened horses met Catfish in the trail and shied around him, to continue their wild run toward the supposed safety of the corrals. The sight of Catfish hushed up the dogs, who sneaked guiltily off in three different directions, knowing full well that, by rights, Catfish ought to have chunked them with rocks for chasing the horses.

Catfish paid no mind to either horses or dogs. He rushed on down the rocky trail till the sight of Curly trotting toward him down the opposite slope of the creek pulled him up short.

For a moment, Catfish was so overwhelmed with relief that he could neither move nor speak. Then, crying out, he went charging through the shallow water, calling to Curly as he ran.

"Curly!" he implored. "Oh, my baby boy! What on earth has happened?"

He saw Curly bristle at the term "baby boy," and set his jaw stubbornly. He wouldn't say a word till Catfish had run up and caught him by the arm and shaken him and demanded all over again, "What on earth's happened, Curly? Where's Shinnery Red?"

Curly pulled away from his father and stabbed a thumb back over his shoulder.

"Shinnery's back up on the ridge yonder," he said, then added with a touch of malice, "And what happened is—he got throwed."

Catfish's eyes widened in alarm. "Got throwed? Is he hurt?"

"Aw, I guess them cactus stickers is hurting him some," Curly said. "But it's the hurt to his pride that's giving him the worst pain. I look for it to take him a good long spell to get over that."

"But what *happened?*" Catfish demanded.

Curly said impatiently, "I *told* you he got throwed, didn't I?"

Pushing past his father, Curly waded into the creek crossing, headed toward the house.

Confused, hurt by Curly's impatience, Catfish stammered, "Yeah—b-but wait, now. Where you fixing to go?"

Curly kept going, answering without looking back, "I'm fixing to go after that fool horse and them rattle-brained dogs. I've still got me a wild hog to catch!"

Completely bewildered, knowing little more than the fact that his boys were still alive, Catfish stared after his younger son with an anxious look on his face. He wished he knew what had happened, but there didn't seem to be any way of getting that information out of Curly. He wished he had enough control over the boy to persuade him not to go after that bad hog a second time; but he didn't have that control, and following along and begging wouldn't do any good. As sore at Shinnery Red—and the world in general—as Curly was right now, a man trying to reason with him might just as well be hollering straight into a big wind.

Catfish's troubled mind switched then to Shinnery Red. He thought some of going to see if his older son might need his help in any way, but finally discarded that idea, too. If Shinnery was feeling sensitive about getting thrown from that bronc horse, he sure wouldn't appreciate a fumbling old man showing up to shame him with a lot of fool questions.

In fact, after looking the situation over from every possible angle, Catfish finally decided that the best thing he could do was go on back to the house and sit with his jug again.

The jug, of course, wasn't going to solve any of his problems on how to keep a couple of mule-headed boys from killing themselves. Still, if a man didn't know a blessed thing about raising boys and was fretting himself sick about it, a little nip now and then could be a big comfort.

Six

AT Curly's urging, the hound, Liverpill, picked up the boar's trail at the corner of the field and led off. Coalie and Half-Pint ran with him, with Curly, once more mounted on Midnight, following close behind. For some three or four miles, over sharp rocky ridges, down brush-covered slopes, and across gullied dry watercourses, the dogs ran the trail with joyous abandon. But once they'd brought the boar to bay a second time, their eagerness subsided.

As before, the rangy old boar had picked his own spot in which to make a stand. He'd backed up under an overhanging lip of rock in the curving bed of a dry wash. The bank protected his sides and rear, while a stand of scrub cedar growing a few yards out in front of his retreat stood just tall enough to prevent Curly's roping him. Also, the brush stood thick enough to discourage the dogs from making a direct frontal attack.

The cagy old boar knew he had himself another

tight nest to protect him from his enemies, so he walked proudly back and forth on tiptoe, roaring his defiance. He'd completely routed this bunch one time, and there was no question in his mind but what he could do it again. He snapped suggestively at thin air, popped vicious teeth, and boldly dared the outfit to bring the fight to him any time they could rake up the nerve.

Nobody felt ready to tackle him for a good long while. The baying dogs kept their distance, and so did Curly.

Curly rode a half circle around the roaring hog, searching for an opening between the cedars through which he might cast his loop. He couldn't find one. Disappointed and frustrated, he sat his saddle for a while, shouting all sorts of ugly insults at the boar; but the old hog didn't seem to take offense.

Stirred by a grudging admiration for the nerve and sagacity of the hog—a feeling the boy would have hotly denied if anybody had accused him of it—Curly at last got down and tied Midnight to a live-oak sapling.

"Now try to run off and leave me afoot again," he challenged.

Taking down his rope, Curly climbed the ledge.

From the shelf of rock under his feet, he had to bend far over even to see the boar. To rope him from that angle would be impossible.

Curly considered. He studied the boar for a while, then straightened up and looked at the dogs.

"Git him, Coalie!" he shouted suddenly. "Crowd in on him!"

He didn't expect the dogs to catch the boar. All he wanted them to do was crowd in close enough that the boar would charge them. He ran out a loop and got set for a throw and kept urging the dogs.

"Rush him!" he yelled. "Bring him out into the open."

The trick worked. The boar watched the reluctant dogs pressing closer through the cedars, and his rage increased. He thought he saw a chance to get in a killing lick. Uttering a roar of defiance, he quit the protection of the shallow cave in a lightning-swift charge.

He made a perfect target for Curly. The boy swung his rope aloft like an old hand at the game. The loop leaped out ahead of the hog and stood open for the tiny fraction of a second necessary for the boar to run into it. Then Curly hauled back on the rope, yanking the loop shut around the boar's shoulders and between his front legs, the only way to keep a rope on a hog.

Curly had him a wild boar caught.

The only trouble was, Curly had caught more boar than he could handle. He simply didn't pack enough weight in the seat of his pants to stop a two-hundred-pound wild hog charging full tilt.

The hog hit the end of the rope like a runaway train. Curly's heels flew up, and he turned tail end over appetite. He piled up in the rocky bottom of the wash with a jolt that rattled his teeth and knocked the breath clear out of him.

For an instant, Curly was too stunned to move, and that instant proved too long. Already the enraged boar had wheeled about. Curly caught a blurred glimpse of the hog already charging him.

Frantic with fear, Curly lunged to his feet. He tried to leap out of the path of that murderous charge and knew the sudden wild terror of being too slow and too late.

With a triumphant roar, the boar hit Curly about the bend of the knees, upsetting and slamming him to earth again.

It was Curly's loud scream that brought in the dogs. That cry aroused in them a protective instinct that no normal fear could quell. They came raging in with white fangs bared. They swarmed all over the boar, slashing with a fury that disregarded all consequences.

The fight whirled around Curly, then over him. The screaming roar of it was in his ears. The rank blood stench of it was in his nostrils. Hard hog hoofs gouged into his ribs and raking dog claws ripped his shirt to shreds. Then he was up and staggering about in a boil of dust that all but hid the fight.

The dogs had no chance in such close quarters.

Above their wild baying and the roar of the enraged boar, Curly heard Coalie's cry of pain.
Gripped by a nightmare paralysis, Curly stood
stock-still and watched the black shepherd come
rolling out of the fog of dust. The screeching dog
landed against the butt of a cedar, where he lay flat
on his back, pawing the air frantically. Curly stood
appalled at the sight of the dog's bleeding belly,
laid open to the hollow.

A second later, the hound, Liverpill, was caught
against the rock ledge and cut down. Without
checking his charge, the boar rushed straight
ahead, and Curly barely leaped aside in time to
escape a like fate.

The boar didn't stop to whirl again. Before him
stood the black horse, Midnight, snorting and rearing and falling back against the reins that held him
tied to the live oak.

To the angry boar, Midnight was just another
enemy in his path; he drove toward him with
deadly intent.

If he expected an easy victory here, he got a big
surprise. Midnight saw him coming. He squatted
and flattened his ears. Then, with a squeal of terror, he lashed out viciously with both hind feet. He
missed with one foot, but the other iron-shod hoof
struck the boar squarely between the eyes and
popped loudly against the bone.

The blow reeled the boar back on his rump and

sent him rolling, as he had rolled the dogs. He came to a stop and lay still for a moment, then scrambled slowly to his feet. Blood oozed from his ears and snout. He stood and stared at the snorting Midnight, as if he couldn't quite understand or believe what had happened. Finally, he moved off into the brush, uttering short grunts of pain and bewilderment. He swayed as he walked, weaving and staggering about like a Saturday night drunk.

Seven

———

SHINNERY Red was mad enough to bite nails when he came crippling up to the cabin where his father sat in his rocking chair. There were still cactus spines in Shinnery's hide that he couldn't reach to pull out and he was in no mood to answer a lot of questions as he stalked across the corner of the gallery and headed for the corral. But, like he'd expected, his father couldn't let him alone. He had to get up out of his chair and hurry after his long-striding son, spouting questions by the mouthful.

"You bad hurt, son?" Catfish wanted to know.

"Course not," Shinnery said, without halting or looking around. "What makes you think I'm hurt?"

"Well," Catfish said, "it's just that Curly says you got throwed."

Shinnery turned on his father. There was such black anger in his face that Catfish halted and backed up a step.

"The little devil's lying!" Shinnery shouted. "I didn't *get* throwed. Curly *got* me throwed!"

Catfish stared uncertainly at his angry son, not quite able to make a clear distinction between Shinnery's *not* getting thrown and Curly's *getting* him thrown.

"Well," he faltered, "I didn't aim to make you mad. Just wanted to know what happened."

"It don't matter what happened," Shinnery Red declared. "It's what's gonna happen that counts. Where is Curly, anyhow?"

"Why, he went off to hunt that old hog again," Catfish said. "Wish he'd let that rascal alone. Before *he* gets hurt."

"He'd have gotten a heap worse hurt," Shinnery said, "if he'd been here and I ever get my hands on him."

"Now, son," Catfish protested. "You wouldn't want to do Curly no harm. Him your little brother and all."

Shinnery snorted. "I'd as soon have a diamondback rattler for a little brother. Be safer to love."

With that, Shinnery Red strode angrily toward the corral. There, the bay horse snorted and shied away from him. Shinnery leaped forward, bent, and grabbed up the dragging hackamore rope, then threw his weight against it, halting the bay.

His father came running in to pester him further.

"You surely ain't fixing to ride that killer horse again!" Catfish cried.

[56]

"Course I'm fixing to ride him!" Shinnery flared. "How else you think I can break him to saddle? And, thanks to Curly, he's gonna be a whole lot meaner and harder to ride than he's ever been before."

"But he's done throwed you once," Catfish protested. Catfish was nearly in tears.

Shinnery turned savagely on his father. "And I done told you different! Curly jumped him out from under me when I wasn't looking. But he ain't throwed me; he can't throw me; and if he's got the least notion left in his head that he can throw me, I'm fixing to knock that out of him right now!"

Shinnery saw his father's face blanch with fear. He dodged quickly as Catfish yelled, "Look out!" He flung himself to one side barely in time to escape the flailing forefeet of the bay, who had reared and was trying to chop his brains out. He hauled down on the hackamore rope, bringing the fighting horse back to earth, then shouted angrily at his father, "Pa, will you get out of this pen before you get us both killed?"

Catfish backed up, aware that his presence had distracted his son's attention at a crucial moment.

He said in apology, "I didn't aim to interfere— I just—" then flinched as Shinnery Red lashed out at him again.

"Well, then get outta here. Like I said!"

Fuming with rage, Shinnery turned his attention

[57]

to the horse. He crowded in beside the snorting animal, pulling the rascal's head down and around till he could get his hand on the saddle horn and one foot in the stirrup. Then, quick as a cat, he went up and across. He felt a rising saddle slap him hard in the seat and clamped himself solidly into it, then slammed home the spurs.

It was like trying to ride a cyclone with the bridle off. The angry bay leaped high under him, dropped back to earth so hard that Shinnery Red felt the jolt shoot all the way up his backbone. The bronc put everything he had into wild careening leaps that rattled every bone in Shinnery's body. Wheeling and bawling, pitching and squawling, he circled the corral a couple of times. Then, ignoring a wide-open gate, he attempted to leap the picket-pole fence and all but turned a wildcat as he crashed through the top of it, sending splintered pickets flying in all directions.

All that kept Shinnery Red in the saddle was a grim determination to conquer and a willingness to grab mane or claw leather or do whatever else it might take to hold him on. So he was still up in the middle of the bay when the horse finally threw up his tail and called it quits. But the rider was hurting all over and his head was buzzing, and when he stepped to the ground, he was seized by a reeling dizziness so sickening that he hardly had the strength to unbuckle his cinch and drag his saddle rigging from the bay's sweaty back.

And it sure didn't help his feelings any to look up about then and see his brother, Curly, riding toward the corral. Curly's hat was gone. His head was skinned. His shirt had been torn to ribbons. He rode with the bridle reins clenched between his teeth, and under each arm he held a whimpering, bloody dog.

That one glance told Shinnery that Curly had tied into his boar hog and got bested again. And right then, Shinnery Red felt just mean enough to be glad of it. Confound it! It was Curly's fault that he'd taken such brutal punishment from the bay horse. If Curly hadn't lost his temper and hurled that stick at him, there would have been no call for the bay to throw such a wall-eyed fit.

Eight

WILD with apprehension, Catfish ran to meet the bedraggled Curly.

"Curly!" he cried out. "Gosh dog, baby! You bad hurt?"

For once, Curly didn't seem to resent the term "baby." He said in a strained voice, "It ain't me, Pa. It's the dogs."

Catfish saw tears in Curly's eyes and felt a rush of sympathy for the boy.

"Aw, maybe they ain't hurt so bad," he said. "Hand 'em down and let's see."

He lifted his arms to receive the hound, and Shinnery Red came up on the other side and lifted down Coalie.

Shinnery gasped at the sight of the shepherd's ripped belly. "Ain't hurt bad!" he said angrily. "Why, poor old Coalie here, he's cut wide open."

Catfish shook his head at the sight of Liverpill's wound and looked up at Curly. "What happened, son?" he asked gently.

[61]

Curly had to swallow twice before he could answer. "The dogs—they pitched in to save me and—"

Shinnery Red snorted. "It's easy to see what happened," he said. "Curly got himself into a jackpot with that boar hog. And the dogs had to pay to get him out."

"Guess you was there!" Curly flared.

"I oughtta been," Shinnery flared back.

"Sure!" Curly sneered. "So you could set and watch and laugh your fool head off. And not turn a hand to help out."

"Here, here, now," Catfish put in. "We got no time for a fuss. These dogs is hurt bad and need patching up."

Holding Liverpill in his arms, Catfish turned toward the house. "Let's take 'em to the smokehouse, Shinnery," he said back over his shoulder. "Where the blowflies can't get to 'em. . . . And, Curly, you go to the house and hunt up a spaying needle and some catgut."

The brothers exchanged looks of hot-eyed resentment, then turned to obey their father.

Curly brought the necessary sewing equipment to the smokehouse, then helped Shinnery hold the dogs while their father did the sewing.

The best they could tell, Coalie's wound, as bad as it looked, was a clean cut. None of the entrails had been punctured. With any luck, the dog would be up and around in less than a week.

Liverpill's wound, though, was something else. The broken tusk of the hog had caught the hound at the point of the shoulder and driven deeply in before tearing its way out through the neck muscles. The jugular vein hadn't been cut, else the dog would already have bled to death. But there was no way of telling what injuries Liverpill might be suffering deeper in. All Catfish could do was sew up the ugly gash, leaving a lower corner of the wound open to drain, and hope for the best.

The dogs winced and whined when the big needle pierced the raw lips of their wounds, but neither lost his head and tried to bite. Both knew that Catfish and the boys were trying to ease their pain, so they whimpered and licked Curly's hands to show how grateful they were.

Half-Pint, who wasn't hurt at all, had to get in on the show. He hovered close by, whimpered when the hurt dogs whimpered, and licked Curly's hands when the others did.

That's what got under Curly's skin so badly—the way those two valiant dogs lay there and licked his dirty hands. Like Shinnery had accused, Curly had acted a fool. And to save him, the dogs had come piling in when they knew they didn't have a chance to come out with whole hides.

Thinking of that, Curly felt hot tears streaming from his eyes, and didn't bother to wipe them away.

Shinnery saw the tears and regretted all the mean things he'd said to his brother. Catfish saw them and felt a dry lump climb up into his throat. He thought how cruel life was and wondered why the Almighty ever made it that way, with so much hurt and pain and disappointment.

Nobody said anything, though. They finished the job, bedded the wounded dogs down on some tow sacks, and went silently into the house.

Curly started building a fire in the cookstove, getting ready to fry the catfish. Catfish went to his jug and took a good drink, then stood thinking for a long moment before he finally turned to Shinnery Red.

"Shinnery," he said, "I want you to ride out with your Winchester and locate that boar hog and shoot him between the eyes. I'd do it myself if I could hit the broadside of a house with the winders all shut."

Curly wheeled angrily away from the stove. "No!" he said heatedly. "Shinnery ain't going to shoot that hog and you ain't either, Pa. The difference is between me and him. I said I'd get the big devil and I'll get him. But now it ain't because of my watermelon. It's for what he done to Coalie and Liverpill."

Catfish looked uncertainly about, took another drink, and stood with his head down in deep study. Finally, he said, "Well, now, Curly, you don't want to get into too big a lather about them dogs getting cut up on your account. They done what they figured they had to do. Every critter's got a right to love something enough to die for it, and that's the way Coalie and Liverpill felt about you. They wouldn't have had it no other way."

Curly's tears started again. His chin went to quivering. "Well, y'all heard what I said," he said desperately. Then he went rushing out of the room.

Catfish started to follow, but Shinnery Red caught him by the arm.

"Now, hold on, Pa," he said gently. "You'll shame him. Curly's got some out-loud bawling to do, and he'll want to do it alone. I always did."

Catfish studied on that a moment, then nodded. "You're right, Shinnery," he said. "But we're sure gonna have to watch after him for a spell. Especially if one of them dogs dies."

"We'll watch him," Shinnery said. "I won't hardly let him out of my sight till he gets over it."

Nine

FOR the next couple of days, nobody around the Waggoner cabin had much to say. Shinnery Red saddled and rode the bay a time or two, but the bronc didn't put on much of a show. He pitched some, but more to save his pride than with any real notion of throwing his rider. The battle he'd lost to Shinnery Red the day the dogs got cut up had taken most of the fight out of the bay.

Catfish spent his time sitting out on the front gallery of his cabin, rocking in his chair, taking an occasional nip from his jug. He hoped the raw spirits would numb his mind against his worry about Curly and the boar hog, but they didn't. In fact, they soured on his stomach and made him feel more depressed than ever. So he quit drinking and tried to face up to the problem like the strong man he'd always wanted to be.

He knew men with minds like steel traps. They could size up a situation like this, call the turn, and never look back. One would say, "Curly, if I catch you messing with that wild boar hog again, I'll bust your tail. You hear me?" Or another would say, "All right, Curly, if you want to act a butt-head, just go on and tie into that boar and take your chances." And in either case, that would be final, and they wouldn't worry and fret over it any more.

The trouble was, Catfish didn't have a steel-trap mind. His mind was like a fishnet with big holes in it; anything could go through it and generally did. He couldn't for the life of him seize upon a single idea and stay with it. He'd think one minute, "Well, gosh dog! Of course Curly's mad at that boar hog. I'd be mad, too. The boy's got a right to run that devil down, after what he done to his watermelon and them dogs." But a minute later, Catfish would be thinking, "But that boar hog could gut him just as quick as he did pore old Coalie!" And that would frighten him so badly that his mind would flee from it and search frantically about for more peaceful thoughts, like catfishing. But before Catfish had time to consider what sort of bait he'd like to use next, his mind would go back to worrying about Curly again.

Catfish wasn't the best example of what some people like to call "a man of decision."

As for Curly, he was so torn with pangs of remorse that he could think of nothing else. He hung around the smokehouse, watching over the dogs, bringing them water, and doctoring their wounds, till finally Shinnery Red had to call him down on it.

"Look, Curly," he said, "you're worrying them with too much attention. Better let them alone so they can rest."

The best they could tell, the hound was worse on the third day. He lay stretched out on the floor, hot with fever and barely breathing. By the middle of that afternoon, Curly could stand it no longer. He caught Shinnery Red not watching and saddled Midnight and rode out into the hills. He wasn't going anywhere, especially. He just couldn't stay there and watch Liverpill die.

He was back up Mud Spring Hollow when he ran across the worm-infested shoat. The tormented pig came reeling down the trail to meet him. He was trying to make it to water, where he might soak out the worms, but was too blinded with pain to see where he was going. All of one ear had been eaten away by the parasites that kept boring deeper into his head. Blood trickled down the side of his jaw and leaked from his snout.

Curly eyed the wounded shoat speculatively. Might be, he ought to knock it in the head. A scrub shoat like that, if he was well and fat, wouldn't be worth but a mighty little money. Still, a body couldn't sell a dead shoat for anything; and part of looking after a hog and cow ranch was seeing to it that the screwworms didn't eat up every critter on the place. Curly guessed he might as well catch the shoat and take him home for doctoring.

He didn't bother with a rope. He just stepped down off his horse and caught the pig by its hind leg and tied its feet together with a piggin' string.

That was all simple and easy to do; but loading the squealing shoat on Midnight was another matter. Midnight didn't take to the idea of carrying that pig on his back. He didn't like the scent of it or the squeal of it or the sight of it. He snorted and reared against the reins, like maybe Curly was approaching him with a live rattlesnake.

Curly lost his temper. "Hold still, you old fool!" he shouted.

He tried to haul Midnight's head down so that he could get a foot into the stirrup. But it was no use. The closer he got, the more frightened Midnight became.

Curly finally saw that the black didn't mean to let him climb aboard with the pig. He held the reins in one hand and the squealing shoat in the other and stared around, trying to figure what to do. His eye lit on a broken blackjack-oak snag that stuck out over the trail. The branch was about head high. Maybe if he hung the shoat up on the snag, he could mount Midnight and ride him under it.

He tied Midnight to a bush. He stood on tiptoe and had to use both hands to lift the starved shoat that high, but finally hung him up in the tree. Then he went back and mounted Midnight.

Midnight was still snorty. But the pig had quit squealing for a moment; so Curly managed to spur the horse under it. Gently, he lifted the pig down and hung its crossed legs around the saddle horn. But at the first movement of the horse under him, the shoat let out another terrified squeal. And that's when Midnight fell to pieces.

The black snorted and leaped ten feet to one side, landing in the fallen top of a dead Spanish oak. He stumbled, went almost to his knees, then righted himself and reared high on his hind legs.

"Whoa, confound you!" Curly shouted.

He struck Midnight a heavy blow between the ears with his doubled-up fist, trying to knock him back down.

But he couldn't hit hard enough. Too late, he saw that Midnight was coming over backwards on him. He tried then to quit the saddle, but his right spur hung in a crooked branch of the treetop and held him. He felt a spasm of fear. He'd be crushed to death beneath the rearing horse. He kicked frantically to free his spur, leaning far out of his saddle on the other side. Nothing did any good.

They landed with a grunt and a crash of breaking branches and all four of Midnight's feet in the air. The saddle horn gouged the ground beside Curly's ribs, holding the bulk of Midnight's weight off the boy. The black rolled sideways, pinning Curly's left leg against the ground.

[71]

It was the first time Curly had ever had a horse down on him, but it wasn't the first time he'd ever seen one down on a man. Shinnery Red broke horses for a living, and he'd told Curly what to do in a case like this.

"Grab the saddle horn and hold him down," Shinnery had always said. "You ever let him up, he'll stomp you to death, trying to get back on his feet."

Curly felt the crushing weight on his leg increase as the struggling Midnight tried to get to his feet. Frantically, the boy grabbed the saddle horn with both hands and just barely had weight enough to hold the animal down. Midnight squealed, and his flailing feet shattered the dead Spanish-oak top, clearing the brush away and filling the boy's eyes and mouth with shreds of bark and dust. But Curly held grimly to that saddle horn.

Finally the horse ceased his struggles, and they lay there in a deadlock—Midnight unable to get up, Curly unable to withdraw his leg. Just behind Curly lay the tied-up shoat, squealing at the top of his voice.

They lay that way for a long time—for hours, it seemed like to Curly, who felt his leg growing numb under the weight of the horse and wondered if it were broken. They lay there, with Curly getting madder by the minute at Shinnery Red. Wasn't it just like grownups, and his brother especially, he thought, to act wise and biggety while delivering a piece of advice that wasn't worth one red copper cent without more information.

Sure! Holding a horse down so he couldn't get up and stomp your guts out, that was just fine! But then what? Who's going to come along and help you get out from under him? And if somebody is coming, how long is it going to take them to get there?

Curly lay there, pondering these problems, and got so mad that he was ready to cut slits in Shinnery Red's big ears and then run his brother's feet through the slits. He guessed that, caught in the same fix, Shinnery Red would have time to do some thinking, himself. Then maybe he could do his fool laughing on the other side of his big mouth!

About then, Midnight snorted again and renewed his efforts to get up, scrambling with frantic urgency this time.

Curly held the saddle horn with one hand and reached out with the other toward a fist-sized chunk of rock that lay in front of him. He had the idea that if he could knock Midnight in the head and stun him, he might could pull his leg free.

The rock lay just beyond his fingertips. He strained farther, then changed hands on the saddle horn to reach with his right one. Out of the corner of his eye, he caught a slinking animal movement. He halted his groping then to take a closer look.

Twenty feet away, a stand of live oaks and mountain elms grew out of a split in the bedrock, shading a bench just above his head. In the shadows of the trees crouched a catamount!

Curly froze. Midnight continued to snort and sling his head. The pig kept squealing. The big tawny cat crept forward a couple of steps and flattened again. His baleful yellow eyes stared straight into Curly's, and the tip end of his long, ropelike tail twitched from side to side.

Curly had considered his predicament plenty desperate as it was. Now he realized that he was in greater jeopardy. He knew that "Mexican lions" were cowardly creatures and not in the habit of attacking a man. On the other hand, he could tell that this one was fixing to attack. It was plain to Curly that the big cat had him and the horse figured for cripples who would be easy prey. Or maybe it was the squealing pig that he was after. It didn't really matter. Once that big devil raked up the guts to spring, he'd rip to pieces everything that moved under his mighty claws.

For an instant, panic got the upper hand of Curly. He tried to scream. But if any sound came from his throat, he couldn't hear it above the constant shrill squealing of the shoat.

Curly sucked in a quick breath and got a grip on himself. This was a game for keeps. He had better think fast and call the turn right; there were no

dogs to save his hide this time. He'd wind up as cat bait and that would be the end of Curly Waggoner.

For one faint-hearted moment, Curly longed desperately for the sight of his brother, Shinnery Red, then resolutely put that thought out of his mind. If by some miracle his brother were to appear, he'd probably just sit around and laugh at the fix Curly had gotten himself into.

Curly considered first the idea of letting Midnight get to his feet while he took his own chances of getting out from under. Then he had another idea. He reached again for the rock he'd been after. He failed to get it, but his fingers closed over a foot-long piece of seasoned Spanish oak.

With an awkward movement, he hurled the stick at the lion. The big cat dodged nervously to one side, snarled, and slapped at the stick, spinning it away. Then he turned back to face his prey, and his coughing roar was loud above the squealing of the shoat.

That's when Curly caught sight of the black boar.

Ten

THE big killer hog came crashing out of the brush with a roar. His bristles stood up along his backbone like the teeth on a wire comb. He ran with his head held high and his mouth half open, exposing every tooth in his jaws. He came on tiptoe, and his onrush carried him straight for the catamount.

The cat slunk sideways in fright. When he saw that he couldn't escape, he squawled and flung himself into the air to meet the assault.

They tangled not ten feet from where Curly lay with his leg pinned under the struggling Midnight. The cat landed on the hog, raking with bared claws, almost covering him. But an instant later, the infuriated hog was out from under and the catamount was rolling over and over, spitting and screaming and biting at a long bloody gash across his ribs.

The boar wheeled swiftly about and charged again, uttering a roar of defiance. His blood-lust was up; he was out for a kill. The yowling cat met the rush and raked long, bloody furrows down the hog's shoulders, but a lightning-swift sideways thrust of the boar's head drove the broken tusk into the cat's neck up to the hilt.

The cat squawled again, flung himself aside, then reared up with blood spouting from his neck. On his hind feet, he doubled over and slapped strutted claws into the hog's rump.

The blow only served to whirl the boar around for a faster charge. And this time, he got in the lick he wanted. He went directly under the outflung claws and drove his broken tusk deep into the cat's soft belly. The cat wrapped himself around the hog, biting and clawing frantically. But it was no use. The boar had the full weight of the cat on that splinter of tusk. He lunged around, slinging the cat from his back and opening the creature's belly the full length.

The cat landed in tall grass. He doubled up in a frenzy of pain, wallowing and snarling, clawing and biting at the wound, tearing out his own vitals. The boar halted, popping his teeth, and watching the cat. Then he turned to face Curly and threaten him with a deep, rumbling roar.

A rifle shot crashed behind the paralyzed Curly. The catamount's head snapped up, then flopped back into the grass to lie still. The pig stopped squealing. Pop-eyed with fear, Curly twisted his head around.

[78]

What he saw made him nearly faint with relief.

It was Shinnery Red, standing on the ground while he levered another cartridge into the shell bed of his rifle. Near him, Catfish, still mounted, was fighting to hold the reins of the spooked bay bronc.

The sight of Shinnery lifting the rifle to his shoulder for a second shot broke the paralysis on Curly. He cried out, "Don't, Shinnery. Don't shoot that boar hog!"

Shinnery hesitated, looked at Curly in astonishment. "You lost your mind?" he demanded. "If the pig ever squeals again, that boar'll rush you!"

"All right," yelled Curly. "Then shoot the pig. He's worm-et till he's liable to die. If he don't, he still ain't worth one bristle on that boar hog." Curly's voice rose to a shrill pitch. "I'm warning you, Shinnery! Don't you shoot that boar hog!"

Shinnery Red sent a questioning glance toward his father, then quickly squinted along his sights toward the rumbling boar that stood popping frothy teeth. He might not understand what Curly had on his mind, but he entertained no doubts about that boar's intentions. One false move, and the killer hog would go on the rampage again. And Curly wouldn't have the chance of a red ant trapped in a doodlebug hole.

"But, Curly . . . look, baby!" Catfish protested, then shrank back as the enraged Curly screamed at him, "Don't call me no baby! And don't let Shinnery shoot that hog, you hear?"

Catfish looked around in bewilderment. He couldn't figure Curly's way of thinking, but guessed there had to be some mighty strong reason behind it. He nodded toward Shinnery.

"Play it his way, Shinnery," he said. "Shoot the pig."

Shinnery swung his rifle about to aim at the pig. "Well, keep a tight grip on that saddle horn," he told Curly.

The Winchester's report cracked like a whiplash in the canyons. The wounded pig jerked, then slumped without uttering a sound. Shinnery reloaded hastily, keeping an eye on the boar, ready to shoot again.

However, the rifle shot seemed to change the boar's mind about charging Curly and Midnight. He ceased popping his teeth. He stared at Shinnery Red for a moment, then began to ease back toward the brush, sniffing loudly.

A moment later, Catfish had swung down out of the saddle, and he and Shinnery Red rushed to where Curly lay under the fallen Midnight.

"You drag him out, Pa," Shinnery Red ordered, "while I let this horse up."

Catfish caught his son under the armpits. Shinnery grasped the black's bridle reins. He pulled the animal's head as far back toward the saddle as he could and told Catfish to be quick about jerking Curly free.

Catfish nodded. "I'm ready when you're ready," he told Shinnery.

"All right," Shinnery Red said. "I'm letting him up."

Shinnery gave the reins slack. Midnight rolled to his knees with a snort and surged to his feet, stamping and kicking. But already Catfish had dragged Curly free of the deadly hoofs.

Face gray with anxiety, Catfish laid his younger son to the ground and hovered over him, feeling Curly's leg.

"Is it broke, baby?" he cried. "Is your pore little old leg broke?"

Curly gritted his teeth for a long moment to hold back his usual resentful retort. Finally, he smiled gravely up at his father.

"Pa," he asked, "do you just have to call me 'baby'?"

Catfish started guiltily. Shinnery Red laughed aloud.

"Some baby!" he said.

"You shut up!" Curly snapped.

Catfish looked ready to cry. "Well, look, Curly," he stammered. "I know you're too big for a name like that. So is Shinnery Red. But, doggone it—I'm getting to be an old man, and you boys—well, you're just all the babies I got left!" With eyes that begged them to understand, Catfish looked apologetically from one son to the other, then away.

The look sobered both boys.

Shinnery moved up to examine Curly's leg. Gently, he ran a hand along it. He asked in a voice of genuine concern, "You think it's bad hurt, Curly?"

Slowly, fearfully, Curly drew up his leg till the bent knee was against his stomach. A thousand prickling pinpoints of pain stabbed his muscles, but there was no feeling of injury. Grinning, he rose suddenly and stamped his foot against the ground to help renew circulation.

"Aw, heck," he declared. "Ain't nothing wrong with that leg. Except that fool Midnight lay on it till the dang thing went to sleep!"

Eleven

THEY rode toward home with the late sun making their shadows long on the grass. They rode with Shinnery Red's mount snorting and crab-walking, nervous with fear of the rank scent of the cata-mount's hide draped across Shinnery's saddle bow.

Curly said in admiration, "If he'll pack in that fresh cat hide without pitching, you've got him broke."

Shinnery grinned and slapped a horsefly on the bay's neck. "Course I have," he bragged. "Why, inside of a week's time, I'll have him so gentle, a baby could herd ducks on him."

"Which of us babies?" Curly asked slyly.

Catfish said soberly, "What I been puzzling on, Curly, is how come you wouldn't let Shinnery shoot that boar hog. As mad at him as you was, I can't understand it."

Curly started guiltily. He'd forgotten the wounded dogs. His lean face grew tense and he asked in a choked voice, "Liverpill dead yet?"

"Dead!" Catfish exclaimed. "Why, that old biscuit-eater was up on his feet and lapping water when we left. Liable to have a side of bacon dragged down, time we get back."

"Couldn't kill that hound with a chopping ax," Shinnery added.

Relief swelled inside Curly. "Man, oh, man," he burst out. "That sure takes a load off my back. If him or Coalie had died, I'd have been ready to go off and cut my throat with a dull knife."

"Well," Catfish persisted, "you still ain't explained why you pawed up so much sand when Shinnery was fixing to shoot that hog."

"Why, gosh dog, Pa," Curly said. "Don't you recollect what you told me? About every critter loving something enough to die for?"

Shinnery Red snorted. "Love!" he said. "In a boar hog? What could one of them stupid things know about love?"

"Hogs ain't so stupid," Catfish declared. "Read it in a book one time. Book listed man as the smartest animal. Then come some of them bobtailed apes. After that, if my remembrance serves me right, the hog was next. Anyhow, he was way up there, close to the top. Which, I reckon, is what makes him so mean and dangerous."

Shinnery Red wouldn't argue the point with his father, but he still wasn't convinced.

Curly said, "Well, I don't know how smart a

hog is. But I tell you, when that old boar heard the pig squealing, he came on the run to save it. Caught scent of the Mexican lion and figured him for the one hurting the pig and tied right into him. Risking his life for it, just like them dogs done for me."

"You still can't call that love," Shinnery Red insisted stubbornly. "Not in a boar hog."

"Call it what you want," Curly said. "It's what saved my hide when that big cat was fixing to jump me. So of course I couldn't let you shoot him. By rights, I ought to go cut a hole in the field fence, where the rascal could go in and eat himself a big bait of watermelon or roasting ears any time the notion strikes him!"

This was exactly the sort of sentimental reasoning to move Catfish to tears. What loyalty! What appreciation! What bigness of heart!

Catfish swelled with pride. His voice was hoarse with emotion as he said to Curly, "Baby, you're true blue! You're like your brother, Shinnery; you got a heart as big as a waterbucket!"

Curly flinched, shot a look of embarrassment at his grinning brother, then grinned back.

"I tell you," Catfish went on, "if your pore dead mama was to step out of them bushes right now, I wouldn't hesitate a minute to say, 'Laurie, you can look with pride on our two babies. There ain't a finer pair in the state of—' "

[86]

"Pa," Shinnery Red interrupted, "you're better at singing."

Catfish looked up, startled. "Singing?" he said.

"Or catfishing," Curly said soberly.

Confused, Catfish looked from one boy to the other, caught the mischief in Curly's eyes, and it pleasured him to know that his boys were poking fun at him.

"All right, dang it," he said, "y'all can just help me bait out that trotline again tonight."

"Me'n Curly's done agreed on that," Shinnery said.

"Gonna use cut-liver bait from that lion," Curly added. "We saved some. It's in Shinnery's morral."

Catfish's eyes widened with surprise. "Why, I never heard tell of baiting with cat liver," he said. "You reckon it'll work?"

"A catfish'll take anything when he's hungry," Shinnery said. "Recollect that big old yellow cat we caught that had swallowed a whole skunk?"

"By dog!" Catfish exclaimed. "I'd forgotten that. Why, we're just liable to snag that old big one tonight."

The glowing prospect set Catfish's blood to racing. By dog! Wouldn't that be something? A night of catfishing with his boys. No trouble on his mind. And maybe landing that old lollapaloosa he'd lost!

He rode ahead, thinking on it till he could no

longer contain his joy. Throwing back his head, he burst into doleful lament:

"Nobody knows the trouble I've seen!
Nobody knows but Jesus!"

Behind him, both boys shuddered. Shinnery shook his head and spoke in a put-upon voice.

"I guess," he said, "I must have heard worse—someplace or other."

Curly nodded. "Me, too," he said, grinning. "But I sure can't think where it was."